Tidy Up, Trevor

Rob Lewis

The Bodley Head
London

Trevor was bored.

   On Monday he'd done a puzzle. On Tuesday he'd been roller skating. On Wednesday he'd painted pictures. On Thursday he'd played tennis. Now Trevor didn't know what to do. In the end, he did nothing.

'Do some digging and weeding,' said his dad.
   'Play with me,' begged his sister.
   'Read a book,' said his mum.
   'Just enjoy yourself, dear,' smiled his granny.

By lunchtime Trevor was still bored. He was bored and grumpy.

Dad was making sandwiches. 'Trevor will help,' said Mum.

'You're not doing anything, are you Trevor?'

'I know just the thing,' said Dad. 'A trip down the river will cheer you up.'

Trevor didn't want to go on a trip down the river.
By now, Mum was fed up too. 'If you're not coming
with us,' she said, 'you can go and tidy your cupboard.'

Trevor wished he had gone on the trip
down the river.

He flumped down on the floor.

The cupboard door swung open, there were
mountains of toys crammed inside. Trevor tugged
at a box. Bump! Out fell a very bouncy ball, a bag
of feathers, a game of Dingy Dungeons, three

jigsaws and a hard brown lump of Plasticine. It would take him a while to tidy up.

Trevor picked up the very bouncy ball. 'I wondered where that was,' he said to himself.

The trip down the river wasn't much fun. No one could forget about Trevor.
'I hope he's all right,' said Mum.

Trevor had found some knotty knitting and
a crumpled kite.

The river curved under deep green leaves. 'I hope
Trevor's being good,' said Dad.

Trevor had found his blue boat and a rubber ring.

It was time to go home. 'I wonder if Trevor has tidied his cupboard,' said his sister.

Trevor had found his train set and racing cars.

Back in the garden, Granny was snoring.
'Has Trevor been good?' asked Dad.
'Oh yes,' yawned Granny, 'as quiet as a mouse.'

'Trevor, we're home!' called Mum.
There was no answer.

'Trevor, what's all this mess?' Mum shouted.
There was still no answer.

The cupboard was tidy.

'Guess what, Mum,' said Trevor. 'I'm not bored any more.'

'Can I tidy up again tomorrow?'